# Angelina Ballerina™
## Dresses Up

I love you ♡ mom and Dad

Based on the stories by Katharine Holabird
Based on the illustrations by Helen Craig

SIMON SPOTLIGHT
An imprint of Simon and Schuster Children's Publishing Division
New York London Toronto Sydney New Delhi
1230 Avenue of the Americas, New York, New York 10020 • This Simon Spotlight paperback edition August 2020 • Illustrations by Robert McPhillips
© 2020 Helen Craig Ltd. and Katharine Holabird. The Angelina Ballerina name and character and the dancing Angelina logo are trademarks
of HIT Entertainment Limited, Katharine Holabird, and Helen Craig. All rights reserved, including the right of reproduction in whole or in part in any form.
SIMON SPOTLIGHT and colophon are registered trademarks of Simon & Schuster, Inc.
For information about special discounts for bulk purchases, please contact Simon & Schuster Special Sales
at 1-866-506-1949 or business@simonandschuster.com • Manufactured in China 0622 LEO
3 4 5 6 7 8 9 10 • ISBN 978-1-5344-6951-8 • ISBN 978-1-5344-6952-5 (eBook)

Angelina Ballerina loves to dance, and when she isn't dancing, she loves to spend the day with Grandma and Grandpa Mouseling. They have so much fun together!

Whenever Angelina visits, Grandma Mouseling lets Angelina try on her straw hat with flowers on the brim. Then Angelina puts on a special apron that's just her size, and she helps Grandpa and Grandma make cheddar-cheese pies for lunch.

Grandpa and Angelina choose lovely roses to put in the flower vase, and Angelina helps set the table for lunch. While they eat, they talk about plans for the afternoon.

Angelina asks, "Please can I play dress-up?" and Grandpa and Grandma smile.

Angelina and Grandma open a very special old trunk. Inside, there are dresses and shoes and gloves and hats that Grandma used to wear when she was a little mouseling. Angelina tries on a beautiful party dress.

"My goodness," Grandma says. "You look like a princess!"

"I feel like a princess!" Angelina says, doing a curtsy. "Next I'm going to try on the green one!"

Angelina has fun trying on everything in the trunk, and Grandma enjoys helping her.

"I sometimes play dress-up at Miss Lilly's house, too," Angelina tells Grandma.

Miss Lilly is Angelina's ballet teacher. She is very kind, and she once let Angelina and Alice, who is Angelina's best friend, try on her collection of ballet costumes, tutus, and even crowns!

"I wish I had a dress-up box of my own!" Angelina says. "I would have ballet dresses and fairy wings and a chef's hat. . . ."

That gives Grandma an idea.

The next week Angelina's grandparents come to visit her, and they bring a big wooden box and paint supplies with them. Grandpa covers the kitchen table with an old cloth to protect it and puts everything on top.

"What is that?" Angelina asks.

"Your new dress-up box!" Grandma says. "You can decorate it however you want, and then we'll make clothes to fill it."

"I've always wanted a dress-up box!" Angelina says excitedly. Grandma and Grandpa look at each other and smile.

Angelina has so much fun painting and decorating her box.

"Ta-da!" she says, when it's all done.
"Lovely, Angelina," says Grandma.
"Good job!" says Grandpa.

Angelina has lots of ideas about what she wants in her dress-up box. Grandma takes her to Miss Thimble's General Store to pick out fabric, buttons, ribbons, thread, patterns, and more.

"We're making clothes for my new dress-up box!" Angelina tells Miss Thimble.

"How wonderful, Angelina! I have something extra for you too," Miss Thimble says, giving Angelina some pretty fabric pieces. "You can keep these in your box to make a skirt or a gown or whatever you can imagine!"

"Thank you!" Angelina says.

Now every time Angelina's grandparents come over, they help Angelina make dress-up costumes. Grandma shows Angelina how to cut a pattern, thread a needle, and sew buttons onto fabric.

When they finally finish making all the costumes, Grandpa puts everything in the dress-up box . . . including the fabric from Miss Thimble.

"Thank you, Grandma and Grandpa!" Angelina says, and she gives each of them a big hug. "I love my dress-up box!"

"I wish Alice and Henry could see this!" Angelina tells them.
"We could play dress-up and have a tea party and . . ."
"A dress-up tea party sounds wonderful!" Grandma says.

Grandma and Grandpa talk to Angelina's parents, and they invite Alice and cousin Henry over to Angelina's house. It isn't long before all three mouselings have picked out special dress-up costumes!

"I'm a doctor!" says Alice.
"I'm a ballet dancer!" says Henry.

"I'm a chef!" says Angelina. "Would you like a cheddar-cheese pie or a cheddar-cheese biscuit?"

"One of each, please," Alice replies.

"Me too!" Henry says.

"What's this?" Alice asks, picking up a piece of fabric from Miss Thimble.

"It's anything you want it to be," Angelina explains.

Alice takes the fabric and wraps it around herself. "This is my gown. Isn't it pretty?"

Henry puts on a cowboy hat and says, "I'm a cowboy, and this is my lasso!"

Angelina adds pretty fabric to her ballet costume and says, "Look! Now I'm Super Angelina Ballerina!"

Angelina, Alice, and Henry help Grandma set the table, and Angelina's mother, father, and baby sister come down to join in the fun.

"We heard there was a dress-up tea party," Angelina's mother says.

"Do you like our hats?" asks Angelina's father.

"Yes, your hats are great!" Angelina says.

"I like your crown and wings too!" Angelina's mother says.

Angelina's father bows, and says, "Princess Angelina Ballerina Fairy, I presume?"

They all sit down for a delicious tea party.

"Thank you for the best dress-up tea party ever, Grandma and Grandpa!" says Angelina.

"You're very welcome, Princess Angelina Ballerina Fairy!" Grandpa and Grandma say, smiling.